Bernadette in the Doghouse

 A LUNCH BUNCH BOOK

Bernadette
in the
Doghouse

Susan Glickman

 Second Story Press

Library and Archives Canada Cataloguing in Publication

Glickman, Susan, 1953-
Bernadette in the doghouse / by Susan Glickman.

ISBN 978-1-897187-92-0

I. Title.

PS8563.L49B49 2011   jC813'.54   C2011-904487-0

Edited by Yasemin Ucar
Designed by Melissa Kaita
Cover and illustrations by Mélanie Allard

Printed and bound in Canada

*Second Story Press gratefully acknowledges the support of the Ontario Arts Council
and the Canada Council for the Arts for our publishing program. We acknowledge
the financial support of the Government of Canada through the Book
Publishing Industry Development Program.*

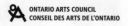

ONTARIO ARTS COUNCIL
CONSEIL DES ARTS DE L'ONTARIO

Canada Council   Conseil des Arts
for the Arts   du Canada

Published by
SECOND STORY PRESS
20 Maud Street, Suite 401
Toronto, ON M5V 2M5
www.secondstorypress.ca

Contents

1

The Dog-watchers

Bernadette Inez O'Brian Schwartz had a long walk to school every morning, a walk that was almost as long as her name. But the time went faster when her friend Keisha Clark, Keisha's big sister Monique, and Keisha's little brother Joshua walked with her. They didn't come by her house every single day because it was a little bit out of their way, but when they did Bernadette was happy because she had a friend to talk with on the way to school, and Bernadette's mother was happy because she got to be with Joshua. She said he was "as cute as a bug's ear," an expression that drove Bernadette crazy because Bernadette was a scientist, and all scientists know that insects don't have ears. Though she often reminded her mother of this important fact, her mother said she liked the expression and kept right on saying it.

Bernadette and her mother also had different ideas about the right way to walk to school. Bernadette's mother and Keisha's big sister Monique liked to walk *s l o w l y* on either side of Joshua so they could swing him over bumps in the sidewalk or puddles when it rained. Bernadette and Keisha thought walking slowly was boring; instead they marched quickly ahead, pretending to be teenagers going to school on their own. They spent a lot of time pointing out interesting things to each other. Keisha liked to look at houses and people, and Bernadette preferred birds and trees and clouds. But they both loved dogs more than anything else. They even made a list like the one Bernadette's father kept when he went birdwatching, with the name and breed of every single dog they met, and the date when they met it. Their list looked like this:

Boo, Labrador, October 28th
Jazz, Fox Terrier, November 5th
Tulip, Maltese, November 19th

…and so on. Playing with other people's dogs was fun. But what Bernadette *really* wanted was a puppy of her own. A soft little puppy with a wet nose and a happy tail; a cuddly, warm puppy curled up on her feet at night; a speedy, athletic puppy chasing balls and Frisbees in the park. Her parents, who had been against the idea when Bernadette was younger, were beginning to weaken as she got older. These days, when Bernadette begged, "Please, PLEASE, *PLEASE* can I have a puppy?"

her mother sometimes said, "Maybe someday,"
or, "We'll have to think about it," instead of just
"No." And as far as Bernadette was concerned,
"maybe" was more than halfway to "yes."

When Bernadette and Keisha arrived at Garden
Road Elementary School each morning there were
lots of dogs to play with, in spite of the sign saying

"NO DOGS ALLOWED" in big shouting letters. Even the principal, Mrs. Garcia, couldn't help patting some of the dogs that weren't supposed to be there. Everyone at Garden Road Elementary School understood that the dogs that weren't allowed were the *other* kind, the kind that growled at children and made messes in the yard.

The only person Bernadette knew who was afraid of dogs was Keisha's little brother, Joshua. He hid behind Monique's legs whenever one came over to say "Hi" in a friendly doggy way, and he started to cry if even the tiniest puppy tried to lick him.

"Why are you scared of dogs, Joshie?" Bernadette asked him one day.

"Doggies bite."

"Not all doggies bite! Did a dog ever bite you?"

"No."

"Did a dog ever bite anyone in your family?"

"No."

"Did a dog ever bite anyone you know?"

"No."

"So why are you so scared of them?"

"Doggies bite," he repeated. And that was all he would ever say on the subject.

On their walk, Bernadette and Keisha always passed a house with a muddy front yard full of garbage. It belonged to an elderly lady who hardly ever came out of her house. A sagging fence separated the yard from a corner store where kids liked to buy snacks. Even though there was a garbage can sitting outside the store, and even though everyone knew they weren't supposed to litter, some of the kids had gotten into the habit of throwing their chip bags and soda cans over the fence. The sight made Bernadette's mother sad. So one day, Bernadette had a brilliant idea. (Bernadette was famous for having brilliant ideas.)

"We could bring a garbage bag tomorrow and clean up the yard on the way home from school, Mom," suggested Bernadette.

"Isn't that trespassing?" asked Keisha's big sister Monique in a worried voice.

"We could ring the doorbell first and ask for permission," said Bernadette. "Anyway, why would the lady mind us cleaning up garbage? It can't be trespassing to do a good deed!"

"OK, we'll give it a try," said Bernadette's mother. "But I don't want anybody getting cut on a rusty can or a piece of broken glass, so I'm bringing some gloves for you children to wear."

When Bernadette's mother met them at school the next afternoon, she had a garbage bag. She also had several pairs of gardening gloves and a little spade to dig up stuff that was buried in the dirt. At the lady's house, Joshua ran up the stairs to the front door, then found he was too short to reach the bell. So Bernadette picked him up and he pressed the bell for a very long time.

No one answered. Disappointed, they were just about to leave when a strange thumping noise could be heard moving slowly toward the door. Joshua hid behind Bernadette nervously until they heard a voice call out, "I'm coming." When the door opened, a bent elderly lady with white hair and sparkly blue eyes stood there, leaning on a walker.

"What can I do for you children?" she asked, with a friendly smile.

"Well," said Bernadette, who suddenly felt shy, "we noticed that your front yard was getting kind of messy from people throwing stuff into it. Would you like us to clean it up for you?"

"What a lovely offer! Thank you so much, my dear. To be honest, I am embarrassed about the way the yard looks. But my arthritis is so bad, I had to give up gardening."

Bernadette's mother came up the walk and joined them.

"How do you do?" she said. "I'm Alice Schwartz. This is my daughter, Bernadette, and our friends Monique, Keisha, and little Joshua here. I hope you don't think the children were rude."

"It's never rude to offer to help somebody," the lady said. "I wish there were more people like you! My name is Helen Marsh, and if you ring the doorbell again when you're finished cleaning up, I just might have some milk and cookies for you."

A half-hour later the front yard was all tidy, and the clean-up crew was enjoying the snack. Mrs. Marsh might have stopped gardening, but she hadn't stopped baking. She had three kinds of cookies for them—chocolate chip, oatmeal raisin, and peanut butter. And as Keisha said, they were three kinds of delicious! Mrs. Marsh also had a beautiful cocker spaniel named Lady, who was lying on a dog bed in the kitchen.

"She's so soft," said Bernadette, stroking Lady's long silky ears. "Aren't you, Lady? Joshie, come feel the doggy's ears. She won't hurt you."

"Doggies bite," he insisted, with his mouth full.

"Lady has never bitten anybody, I promise you," said Mrs. Marsh.

S l o w l y, Joshua came over to look at the dog with his big brown eyes opened wide. Lady thumped her tail on the floor a few times, then got up and pushed a wet nose into Joshua's knees. Joshua put one hand hesitantly on the dog's head before running back to his sisters.

"See? She likes you!" said Keisha.

"This is the closest he's ever been to a dog in his whole life!" said Monique. "Can we come back and visit you and Lady sometime?"

"You will always be welcome," said Mrs. Marsh.

After that, they made it part of their routine to visit Mrs. Marsh and Lady at least once a week. And little by little, Joshua started to overcome his fear of dogs. He wasn't an official dog-watcher yet, but they were pretty sure he would become one, just as soon as he learned how to spell "cocker spaniel."

2

Lights, Camera, Latkes!

Lady wasn't the only new dog in Bernadette's life. Since the middle of November, Keisha had been rehearsing for the Christmas pageant at her church. She was the youngest person in the show and played the part of a heroic puppy. She had rehearsals every weekend, and sometimes she even practiced barking and growling and wagging her invisible tail at school. This annoyed their teacher, Mrs. Hawthorn, but made the other students laugh.

"Keisha," Annie Wang said one day. "You're spending so much time pretending to be a dog you're going to turn into one!"

"If Keisha turns into a dog, maybe my mother will let me adopt her," Bernadette sighed.

"I don't think that *my* mother would let you adopt me, Bernadette," said Keisha, laughing, "but thanks for the thought anyway."

It was the last day before winter break. The girls were sitting in the lunchroom with the fourth member of the Lunch Bunch, Megan MacDonald. The Lunch Bunch specialized in coming up with strategies for enjoying lunch at school. Their strategy that particular day was that everything they ate had to be white, to match the snow piled up outside the windows. So Bernadette had brought vanilla yogurt, a bagel with cream cheese, and a banana (she insisted that the yellow peel didn't count). Keisha had cream of mushroom soup, an English muffin topped with white cheddar cheese, and a container of apple slices (she cut all the peels off carefully so that not even one speck of red was showing). Annie had steamed rice with chicken and cauliflower in it, a container of pears, three arrowroot biscuits, and a bag of popcorn (she was tiny but she always had the biggest lunches). Megan had macaroni and cheese, some green grapes that weren't *quite* white, but almost, on the inside, and a couple of marshmallows just in case the grapes didn't count. (She peeled one grape to show the other girls, and they all agreed that the grapes were pale enough.)

They'd all worked hard, as usual, to make the strategy interesting. But in the end, nobody in the Lunch Bunch cared much about lunch. Since it was the last day of school, Mrs. Hawthorn had promised they could spend the afternoon making a gingerbread house! That sounded like way more fun than eating snow-white food in the noisy lunchroom. Mrs. Hawthorn was also going to read them a story, because even she couldn't concentrate on work today. And after the story, they were going to empty their desks and tidy up the classroom, and that would be that. Two whole weeks of no school stretched before them. Two whole weeks of just having fun.

"I can't wait for the holidays!" said Annie, who was going on a ski trip with her family.

"Me too, because my grandparents are coming next week and my best friend Jasmine is coming the week after," said Bernadette.

"Do you still miss her, Bernadette?" asked Megan.

"Yup," said Bernadette.

"But is she still your best friend?" Megan continued, with a sad face. "What about us? Aren't *we* your best friends now?"

"Of course! You guys are my best friends too," Bernadette replied. "ALL my friends are the best!"

"But Bernadette, that doesn't make any sense,"

said Annie, who was a very logical thinker. "Four different people can't *all* be the best."

"Why not?" asked Bernadette. "Why can't I have four best friends?"

"Because best is at the top. Everything else is underneath," said Annie.

"So if you keep saying that Jasmine is your best friend, it's like telling us that we're not as important to you as she is," said Keisha.

"You know that's not what I mean," said Bernadette. "I love everyone in the Lunch Bunch to pieces! It's just that Jasmine is my oldest friend, and I miss her. That's all."

"Then you should call her your *oldest* friend, and not your best friend, OK?" said Keisha.

"OK," said Bernadette. "I'll try to remember, since it's so important to you." But she didn't feel very comfortable with the discussion, or with the way that Keisha was looking at her. Keisha usually had a smile as bright as sunlight dancing on a fountain. When Keisha smiled, everybody around her just had to smile too. But right then, Keisha looked like a rain cloud.

Jasmine Chatterjee really *was* Bernadette's oldest friend. Bernadette and Jasmine had done everything together since kindergarten, when they discovered that they both loved doing science experiments better than anything else in the whole wide world. They loved doing science experiments more than they loved going to Riverdale Farm to see the new baby lambs and piglets. They loved doing science experiments more than they loved running through the sprinkler on a hot summer day. They even loved doing science experiments more than they loved baking cupcakes and decorating them with ripe red raspberries. And they planned on doing science experiments together until the day they won the Nobel Prize, and even after that!

Bernadette and Jasmine had always sat next to each other in class and they did their homework together after school. Every weekend they took swimming lessons at the community center and had sleepovers at each other's houses. The summer after Grade One, the two families rented a cottage together for a week. During the day they went swimming, and fishing, and canoeing. At night they roasted marshmallows on the fire and then watched shooting stars travel across the sky. Bernadette would have been afraid to be outside at night by herself, because there were bats flying overhead and noises in the bushes that could be hungry bears, or mean pirates, or spooky ghosts. But she was never afraid when she was with Jasmine, because Jasmine wasn't afraid of anything.

Then Jasmine moved away, and Bernadette had been afraid to start Grade Three without her. She had been sure that it was going to be the worst year *ever!* But because of her new friends in the Lunch Bunch, Grade Three was turning out to be a lot of fun. There was always something exciting going on.

The something exciting this week was the Christmas pageant. The whole Lunch Bunch was invited to go on Sunday afternoon with Keisha's family. Keisha looked so sweet dressed as a curly-haired puppy with big brown eyes. She wore a black sweater with a red bow tied around the neck, and black pants with a tail pinned on the back. She even had floppy ears attached to her hairband. Best of all, she didn't make a single mistake saying her lines. When the play was over, the girls clapped so hard their hands hurt, and Keisha's little brother Joshua ran up to the stage and blew her a big noisy kiss, making the audience laugh.

When they left the church it was already dark outside. The street lamps cast a golden glow on the snowflakes that were floating down like big fluffy feathers. Without saying a word to each other, the Lunch Bunch all lay down on their backs and swished their arms up and down to make snow angels. Joshua tried to copy them, except that he wiggled so much his snow angel looked more like

an octopus than a little boy with wings.

"I *love love love* the winter!" sang Annie, and then she caught a big snowflake on her tongue.

"I *love love love* the holidays!" sang Megan, spinning round and around.

"I *love love love* the Lunch Bunch!" sang

21

Bernadette. "And you're all coming to my house on Wednesday because my Bubbe is coming to visit, and she makes the best latkes in the whole wide world."

"What are latkes?" asked Keisha.

"Something special for Chanukah. Something super-dee-duper-deeLICIOUS," said Bernadette.

"More delicious than Christmas pudding?"

"Different delicious. I can't explain; you just have to try them."

"Mmmm! I *love love love* trying new food!" said Annie, biting into a snowball, making everybody laugh.

Bubbe, the famous latke maker, was Bernadette's father's mother. She and Bernadette's father's father, whom Bernadette called Zaide, lived far away, but they came to visit every year during the winter holidays. And during the holidays Bubbe always made latkes—potato pancakes—to eat with applesauce sweetened with sugar and cinna-mon. This year Bernadette asked if Bubbe could make an extra big supply so that she could invite the Lunch Bunch over.

"Of course, Bernadette, I would love to meet your new friends," Bubbe said.

"They're not exactly *new* anymore," Bernadette answered. "We've been together since the begin-ning of Grade Three."

"And how long is that?"

"More than three months!" said Bernadette proudly.

"Well," Bubbe replied, "do you want to know a secret?"

"Sure, Bubbe. And don't worry about me tell-ing anyone. I'm famous for keeping secrets!"

"I have been friends with the same lady since we were eleven years old. That's more than fifty years of friendship. We went to school together, and we lived together during university, and we went to each other's weddings, and we saw each other's children grow up."

"You've been friends for fifty years? Wow! That's almost *forever!* But you know what, Bubbe? I'll bet the Lunch Bunch is going to be friends forever too. You just wait and see."

When they arrived at Bernadette's house, each of the girls in the Lunch Bunch was given a little candle. Bubbe lit Bernadette's, which was red like her hair, and then Bernadette used it to light the others. Megan's candle was blue because she had blue eyes. Keisha's candle was bright yellow because yellow was her favorite color. And Annie's candle was forest green to match the jacket she wore for her gymnastics team. Bernadette had chosen them specially. The girls placed their candles in the menorah, a shiny silver candle-holder, and then Bernadette's family sang a song in Hebrew.

"What does that song mean?" asked Keisha.

"It means that we are grateful for the gift of light, and for having special times to celebrate together," said Bernadette's father.

"In other words, *Lights! Camera! Latkes!*" cried Bernadette.

Bubbe brought in a platter of crispy golden latkes. The girls loved them, especially Annie, who gobbled six whole pancakes before Bernadette had finished eating two. She also drank three glasses of juice and ate a big bowl of salad.

"You must have a hollow leg, young lady," said Bernadette's grandfather, Zaide. "I've never seen such a small person eat so much food!"

"Annie does gymnastics," Bernadette explained. "She's getting ready for a big competition and has to practice three times a week. It takes a lot of energy to do gymnastics, so that's why she's always hungry."

"I knew we could count on you for a scientific

explanation, Bernadette," said Zaide. "Do you still like to do experiments?"

"Yes, she does. Bernadette is famous for science at our school," said Megan.

"Just like Megan is famous for art," added Annie.

"And Keisha is famous for acting," said Bernadette. "You should have seen her in the play on Sunday, Bubbe. She was amazing!"

"I loved that play so much," said Megan. "And I especially loved that a puppy got to be the hero!"

"There are lots of dog heroes," said Annie. "Some rescue their owners by barking when their house catches fire, or by dragging them out of the water to keep them from drowning."

"Dogs are pretty smart," said Keisha. "They can be trained to help blind people and deaf people. They can tell you when the light is green so you can cross the road safely. They can tell you that your phone is ringing. They can bring you your slippers. Plus, they're cuddly."

"Which is why *I keep asking for a dog*," said Bernadette, in a loud voice. "Maybe this is the Chanukah I'll get lucky, and a puppy will magically appear with a bow around its neck and a gift tag saying *For Bernadette*."

"Who wants more latkes?" said Bernadette's mother, changing the subject.

"You're changing the subject, Mom," said Bernadette. "That is definitely not a good sign."

"But Bubbe's latkes are always good, so come and get them while they're hot," said Bernadette's father.

When everyone had eaten as much as they possibly could, they sat on the floor and played the dreidel game, spinning a top to win chocolate coins.

"Chanukah is fun, Bernadette," said Annie.

"Christmas is fun too," said Megan.

"All holidays are fun," said Keisha. "Especially because there's no school!"

"But I like school," Bernadette protested.

"Some school is OK," said Megan. "There's just too much of it. Why do we have five boring days of school and then only two days of the weekend when we can do whatever we want? I think it should be the other way around."

"But if you children weren't at school, who would take care of you while your parents were working?" asked Zaide.

"Well, maybe our parents shouldn't work so much either," said Keisha.

"You've got a point, Keisha," said Bernadette's father, laughing. "Life would certainly be easier if we didn't have to work so hard."

"But if we didn't work so hard, we couldn't afford to buy you Christmas and Chanukah presents," said Bernadette's mother. "So if you had the choice, which would you rather have? More time off school, or presents?"

"Unless the present is a PUPPY, I'm not interested," said Bernadette.

"Oh dear!" said Bernadette's mother. "I'm really in the doghouse now!"

"What does that mean?" asked Bernadette.

"It means that I'm in trouble."

"But what does that have to do with doghouses?" asked Keisha.

"Well, doghouses are usually outside, so sending a dog there means ignoring him when he behaves badly."

"It's OK, Mom. You can stay indoors," said Bernadette. "After all, I'm going to need you here to help me—when I finally get *my* puppy."

"Woof!" said Keisha, wagging her invisible tail.

3

Ice is Nice

Bernadette's grandparents stayed at her house for a
whole week. Bubbe taught Bernadette how to knit
and she made her first scarf. Zaide helped her do a
thousand-piece jigsaw puzzle, and they all played
a bazillion games of Scrabble. One afternoon they
went with Bernadette to have tea at Mrs. Marsh
and Lady's house. They even took Bernadette,
Megan, and Keisha to see a movie. Bernadette had
so much fun with her grandparents that she almost
forgot that Jasmine would be coming for a visit

too. She *almost* forgot—but not quite.

Since Jasmine had moved away, she and Bernadette had become penpals. They wrote real letters with ink on paper and mailed them with pretty stamps—because everyone knows it is way more fun to open up an envelope with your name on it than to get an e-mail on the computer. Their letters to each other sometimes included surprises like lip balm or temporary tattoos or hair clips. For Hallowe'en, Jasmine had sent Bernadette a giant lollipop with a jack-o'-lantern face. And Bernadette once sent Jasmine a pair of socks with frog cartoons on them, because frogs were Jasmine's favorite animals.

But even getting a letter full of loot wasn't as good as being in the same room together talking. So the night before Jasmine's visit, Bernadette couldn't sit still! She tried every trick she could think of to make herself calm down. First she had a bubble bath. After that she put on her coziest pajamas and let her mother comb all the tangles out of her long red hair. Then she drank some hot cocoa, brushed her teeth, and climbed into bed. She put two pillows behind her back, adjusted her lamp, and started reading her favorite book, *The Phantom Tollbooth*. She figured if she tried to read a whole book, her eyes would get so tired they'd close by themselves and **poof**, when she woke up Jasmine would be there, just as if she'd never gone away.

But nothing happened. Bernadette just lay there, watching the glow-in-the-dark hands of her alarm clock go round and round. Five minutes passed. Ten minutes passed. Half an hour passed. She tried the yoga breathing exercises her mom had taught her but they didn't help either. She simply couldn't sleep.

"I simply can't sleep!" Bernadette called out to her parents.

First her mother came in and gave her a cuddle. Then her father came in and sang her a song.

Nothing was working.

"Nothing's working," Bernadette sighed. "I guess I'll just have to stay awake all night."

"Do you know what your Zaide used to do when I was a little boy and couldn't sleep?" asked her father.

"No," said Bernadette. "But I bet you're going to tell me."

"He used to take me outside to look at the moon and stars. He always said that the fresh air would make me tired."

"Did it work?"

"Yes, it really did."

"But I'm already in my pajamas, Dad," said Bernadette.

"Nobody will know that you're wearing pajamas if you put your snowsuit and boots on top of them," said her father.

"But it's so cold outside! And I'm afraid I'll slip on the ice in the dark."

"Don't worry, Bernadette. I won't let you fall."

So Bernadette and her father got all bundled up and went for a nighttime walk. Outside, a deep blanket of snow muffled all the sounds. Snow weighed down the branches of the evergreen trees and sat like a hat on every chimney. Over the white rooftops the sky was a deep endless black. More stars than they could count sparkled in the sky like tiny chips of ice floating on a big dark lake. The moon was so big and bright it seemed closer to the earth than usual.

"Take a deep breath, Bernadette," said her father.

"The air feels prickly!"

"That's because it's freezing the drops of moisture in your breath. How far do you want to walk?"

"Just around the block, Dad. You were right. I'm already starting to feel sleepy."

They walked around the block hand in hand, listening to the snow squeak under their boots.

Bernadette's father stopped to pick a few lacy green needles off a cedar tree and rubbed them between his fingers for Bernadette to smell.

"In the summer we always forget to smell cedar trees because most flowers have stronger perfume," he said. "But in the winter, nothing smells better than this."

They met Sammy, the dog who lived next door, going for his bedtime walk. Sammy was wearing a funny little sweater with a Christmas tree on it and bells that really jingled, and he was so happy to see them that he jumped up to give Bernadette a kiss. *Jingle jingle* went his bells! Then they said hello to another neighbor who was shoveling his driveway. They stopped to admire all the shining decorations on his house. And before they knew it, they were back home again.

"Thanks for the walk, Dad," she said. "It's super cool outside at night. *Cool.* Get it? As in winter?"

"Very funny, Bernadette. But the important thing is, are you ready to go to bed now?" her father asked.

"I can't wait!" Bernadette said, as she peeled off her snowsuit. "Zaide was right. Fresh air really does make you feel tired. And you know what else I've learned? Sometimes, ice is nice."

And she fell asleep as soon as her head touched the pillow.

When Bernadette woke up the next morning she remembered right away what a special day it was.

"Jasmine is coming, Jasmine is coming!" she sang as she ran down the stairs.

"She won't be here for at least two hours," her mother said. "So why don't you eat your breakfast while you're waiting?"

"I'm too excited to eat, Mom."

"Last night you were too excited to sleep, and now you're too excited to eat. Since you have so much energy, Bernadette, you might as well use it to clean up your room."

"On second thought, maybe I could eat just a little teeny tiny bowl of oatmeal with seven or eight raisins and a spoonful of brown sugar and maybe half a sliced banana on top," said Bernadette, slipping into her chair at the kitchen table.

"I *knew* that would work!" her mother laughed.

"Well, *I* knew that you knew that would work," said Bernadette. "I just wanted to make you happy by pretending I didn't."

"Bernadette Inez O'Brian Schwartz! Don't think you can get out of cleaning your room. There will still be plenty of time to do it after breakfast."

"Rats," said Bernadette. "Why are mothers always so bossy?"

After breakfast she went upstairs to clean her room. Jasmine was going to sleep on a spare mattress on the floor beside her bed, so Bernadette wanted everything to be nice and tidy. She pulled up her duvet and folded her pajamas neatly under her pillow. Then she put all her books back on the bookshelves. First she filed them in alphabetical order by topic, so that all her animal books were together, and all her fairytale books were together, and all her plant books were together. Then, within each topic, she filed the books in alphabetical order by their authors' last names. Finally, she dusted her rock collection and arranged the specimens neatly.

Looking at the rocks reminded her of all the times she and Jasmine had gone fossil hunting, and of the geology camp they went to at the museum. They used to do everything together! How could two or three days of holiday make up for all the precious time they'd lost since Jasmine moved away?

Bernadette decided to find a really good experiment for them to do. She was so busy looking through her science books that she didn't even hear Jasmine tiptoe into the room behind her. But suddenly someone's hands covered her eyes, and a familiar voice yelled out, "Surprise!"

"Jasmine! You're here!"

Bernadette dropped the book she was reading, turned around, and gave her friend a big hug.

"No fair, Jasmine, you big cheater!" she said. "You grew another inch since last summer. My nose only comes up to your shoulder now."

"My mom says that because I'm having my growth spurt so young, I'll probably stop growing early too."

"I hope she's right, or I'll *never* get a chance to catch up."

Both girls giggled.

"I missed you so much, Jazzy!"

"I missed you too, Bernie. But at least *you* got

to stay in your old house and keep going to your old school. I had to start everything over again."

"That must have been difficult at first," said Bernadette's mother, coming into the room. "But how is it now?"

"It's good in some ways, and it's bad in others," Jasmine answered slowly.

"What do you mean?" asked Bernadette.

"It's good that we live near my mom's sister and I get to see my cousins all the time. But it's bad that I live so far away from my old friends—especially you, Bernadette. It's good that our new house is bigger than our old one, but it's bad that there's so much traffic that I'm not allowed to cross the road by myself. It's good that my new school has a real laboratory, but it's bad that I don't know French so I have to go to a tutor."

"I see," said Bernadette's mother. "But isn't that how life always is? A mixture of good and bad?"

"Well, there's nothing bad about you being here, Jasmine; it's totally *perfect*," said Bernadette. "And guess what? I just found an amazing experiment for us to do together."

"Yippee!"

"I know you are going to love it. Mom, do we have all these ingredients?" asked Bernadette, picking up the book that had fallen on the floor and flipping through it to find the right page.

"Let me see. Cream? Yes. Vanilla? Yes. Sugar? Of course. And I think we still have some rock salt in the garage; we used it to melt the snow on the sidewalk before we found something better for the environment. So if you girls go outside to get some clean snow, I'll collect everything else you need."

Bernadette and Jasmine put on their coats and boots and mittens and went outside with a big plastic container. It was a sunny day and not too cold, so the snow was sticky.

"Do you want to play in the snow first?" Jasmine asked. "It's perfect for building stuff."

"But I'm tired of making snowmen, Jasmine."

"Well, what about if we make a snow cat?"

"I'd rather make a snow DOG, since I think that's the *ONLY kind of dog I'll ever get around here!*" She shouted this, just in case her mother could still hear them through the closed doors and windows.

"OK, Bernadette. I'll make a cat, and you can make a dog, and then there will be *two* animals running around your yard."

"If we also make a snow mouse, we can have the cat chasing the mouse and the dog chasing the cat."

"And the mouse should chase the dog, so they can run in a circle," said Jasmine.

Building three separate sculptures out of snow took them a long time, but it was worth it.

"Great job, girls," said Bernadette's mother

when they finally went back into the house. "Those animals look fantastic. In fact, I'm going to take a photograph to send you, Jasmine, so you can have a nice memory of this day."

Bernadette's mother got her camera and took some pictures of the snow sculptures, and then she placed two steaming cups of cocoa in front of the two girls.

"Yummy, Mummy," said Bernadette.

"This warms up my tummy!" said Jasmine.

"Do you still want to do that experiment?" asked Bernadette's mother, laughing. "Because it will make you cold all over again. And besides, Bernadette, Keisha called while you were outside, and I told her you'd call her right back."

"I'll call her later, because I still want to do the experiment," said Bernadette.

"Me too!" said Jasmine.

Once they had finished their cocoa, Jasmine brought in a container full of nice clean snow. Bernadette added six tablespoons of rock salt to it and then shook the container for five minutes. It was really cold, so she put oven mitts on her hands to protect them.

"Why don't you wear your real mittens, silly?" Jasmine asked.

"They're soaking wet," Bernadette answered. "Can you keep shaking this thing while I start mixing the other ingredients?"

"OK," said Jasmine, and she put on the oven mitts. While she was shaking the snow and salt mixture, Bernadette stirred a tablespoon of sugar and a half-teaspoon of vanilla into a half cup of cream. Then she poured the liquid into a large zipper lock bag and sealed it tightly, leaving as little air inside as possible.

"The instructions say that we should put this bag inside *another* bag so that the ingredients don't spill, and also to make sure that no salt gets in," Bernadette said. "Can you hold the second bag open for me and I'll slip this one in?"

"Sure," Jasmine replied, putting down her container. "I was sick of shaking that snow anyway. Now what do we do?"

"Now we put the plastic bag of liquid ingredients into the snow container and keep on shaking it for fifteen more minutes."

"But my arms are so tired!" Jasmine moaned. "Can we please take turns?"

"Since you already did five minutes, how about if I do five, then you do five, then I'll do five more."

"It seems like a lot of effort, Bernadette. Do you really think we will end up with old-fashioned vanilla ice cream?"

"Yes, because the salt will help the snow absorb the heat from the cream so the cream will freeze. It's totally *scientific*, Jasmine."

"Well, you know how much I love science. Especially science that tastes good!"

And it did. In fact, it tasted wonderful.

"You're a genius, Bernadette," said Jasmine, licking the last drop of ice cream from her spoon. "This is definitely the best experiment we've ever done."

"I agree. And I have to repeat what I told my dad last night, when we went for a walk in the snow."

"What's that?"

"Sometimes, ice is nice!" said Bernadette, with a big smile.

4

The Friendship Bracelet

The day after the ice cream experiment, Bernadette's father took the girls to visit the Science Center. It was an amazing place full of amazing stuff! The Outer Space area had a rocket ship you could sit in, and a telescope you could look through, and a pretend sky full of twinkling stars. The Planet Earth area had many different habitats full of plants, and small animals like snakes, and lizards, and turtles, and fish. In the Technology area there were all kinds of machines, including a printing press that made real newspapers and a radio that got news from all over the world.

Because they wanted to be scientists when they grew up, Bernadette and Jasmine had already been to the center about fourteen zillion times, but they never got tired of it. Their favorite area was called The Human Body. This was because most of the exhibits let you do fun things like pedal a bicycle until the power made a light bulb switch on, or touch a globe full of static electricity so that your hair stuck straight out like a porcupine's quills. The girls ran around the room happily, trying to identify the smells coming from things hidden inside dark boxes and to feel sound vibrations with their feet. They tested their balance, and their strength, and their vision, and their hearing. They just kept going from one experiment to another until finally Bernadette's father said, "Listen, you two. I've learned all about my reflexes and my heart rate. I've learned about optical illusions and phantom pain. But all that learning has tired me out. I really need a cup of coffee."

"Well, now that you mention it, I am a tiny bit hungry myself," Bernadette answered.

"Me too!" said Jasmine. "In fact, I'm a *lot* hungry."

"That's because you're growing so much, Jazzy," Bernadette said. "Your body is burning a lot of energy. You're a human volcano."

"Should we feed your pet volcano here, or go home where we can make something healthier?" her father asked.

"I'm not ready to go home yet," Bernadette answered. "Please let us eat here, Dad."

"Here's the deal, Bernadette. If you two can put together a nutritious lunch, we'll stay. Otherwise we'll just get something to drink and then go home, OK?" said Bernadette's father.

"What do you think, Jasmine? This sounds kind of *scientific* to me," said Bernadette. "Almost like an experiment!"

"Almost!" said Jasmine. "I'm sure we can find something healthy to eat, even if it's just lettuce and tomatoes on a bun."

In fact, it wasn't that hard to find a healthy lunch in the cafeteria. The hard part was choosing to eat it when there was so much junk food available.

"My brain knows what healthy food is, but my stomach says it wants a hot dog, fries, and a soda," Jasmine said.

"My stomach wants that too," agreed Bernadette. "But my dad won't let us stay if we eat junk food. And I want to stay! So my brain has decided to have a yogurt parfait and a glass of cranberry juice."

"Well, *my* brain has decided on a tuna sandwich on whole wheat with extra pickles on the side," said Jasmine. "And I'll have orange juice to drink, please."

"I'm very proud of you girls," said Bernadette's father, when he saw their tray. "You made excellent lunch choices."

"Unlike you, Mr. Coffee Drinker," said Bernadette. "Why don't you have a glass of milk once in a while?"

"Ouch," said her father. "You're right, Bernadette. We should *all* try to eat healthier."

"Maybe our next Lunch Bunch strategy can be bringing healthier food to school," said Bernadette. "Thanks for the great suggestion, Dad!"

"Bernie," said Jasmine, slowly.

"Yes?"

"I never told you this, but I borrowed your invention. Without asking."

"What do you mean, Jasmine?" asked Bernadette. "What invention?"

"I started my own Lunch Bunch with my new friends. Do you mind?"

It took Bernadette a moment to answer. "I kind of do," she finally admitted. "It makes it seem less special. I mean, I do experiments with *you*, Jasmine. I do lunch strategies with my new friends in the Lunch Bunch. So it's really weird to think of you being in a Lunch Bunch with other people."

"So do you want us to stop doing it?" Jasmine said.

Bernadette looked at her oldest friend, feeling uncomfortable. For a moment, she wished that she could discuss the situation with Keisha, Megan, and Annie, since they were just as much a part of the Lunch Bunch as she was. But they weren't here. And meanwhile Jasmine looked sad, and Bernadette didn't want her to be sad when they were supposed to be enjoying their holiday together.

"No, it's OK," Bernadette said finally. "After all, I didn't invent eating lunch at school, or having friends, or eating lunch at school with friends. I only invented the idea of friends *planning* school lunches together."

"That's very mature of you, Bernadette," said her father. "So mature that, after you girls finish eating, you can each buy a souvenir from the gift shop as a reward."

After lunch, the girls bought matching silver friendship bracelets at the Science Center gift shop and promised to never *ever* take them off. Unless they decided to buy new and better ones after they won the Nobel Prize.

The three days Jasmine stayed at Bernadette's house went by so fast she couldn't believe it! Bernadette's mother took them skating. They made cranberry muffins and caramel popcorn balls. They did an experiment using blotting paper to test the acidity of ordinary food items to see which ones would rot their teeth and explode their stomachs. They *tried* to do an experiment using Bernadette's guinea pig, Hamlet, to see which foods would make him go through a maze of books and pillows faster, but Hamlet wasn't very interested. After going through the maze once and politely nibbling a piece of apple, he got tired of science and just went to sleep on one of the pillows.

"If I had a DOG, I bet *it* wouldn't go to sleep during an *important scientific experiment*," said Bernadette loudly.

"I don't know, Bernadette," said Jasmine. "My cat Shadow will never co-operate when I try to make her do things. At least Hamlet knows a few tricks! I think he's pretty smart."

"He's *very* smart!" Bernadette replied, scooping him up and kissing him on his little pink nose. "I'm sorry if I hurt your feelings, Hamlet. You know how much I love you. It's just that I'm sure you would enjoy having a puppy to play with as much as I would."

They were having so much fun that when Keisha called again to see if Bernadette wanted to sleep over at her house, Bernadette apologized for forgetting to call her back, but said it would have to wait until after Jasmine left. Keisha said she could bring Jasmine with her, but Bernadette still said no. And when Megan called a little later to invite Bernadette and Jasmine to come tobogganing, she said the same thing. She wanted to spend every minute with Jasmine alone. Still, before she was ready to say good-bye to Jasmine, their visit was over. And Bernadette didn't know when she would see her oldest friend again.

"I'm surprised you never had the Lunch Bunch over while Jasmine was here," Bernadette's mother remarked, as she packed Bernadette's lunch for the first day back at school.

"Annie was away most of the time on her ski trip," Bernadette said.

"But what about Keisha and Megan?" asked her mother. "They both phoned here, wanting to see you. Keisha said something about a sleepover, remember?"

"Yeah, I know, but it just seemed too weird to bring my old friend and my new ones together," said Bernadette.

"Why? Did you think they wouldn't get along?"

"No, it's not that . . ." said Bernadette. "It's more that I do different things when I'm with Jasmine than I do when I'm with them, and I just wanted to do *Jasmine*-type things for a few days."

"I understand," said her mother. "Sometimes I feel that way about you! I hardly ever get you to myself anymore, Bernadette."

"Well, that's your own fault for not letting me come home for lunch, Mom," said Bernadette.

"You're not still angry that you have to eat at school every day, are you?"

"No, I'm not angry. But you know that already."

"I do. It's just nice to hear it!" said Bernadette's mom, giving her a big hug. "So, what's the Lunch Bunch strategy for this Friday? Do you have any plans?"

"After seeing the Human Body exhibit at the Science Center, I was thinking about suggesting we all make healthy lunches full of vitamins and stuff. Who knows?" she sighed. "Maybe if I eat enough broccoli, I'll finally get that growth spurt you keep promising me."

But when Bernadette told the Lunch Bunch her strategy, they were not as excited as she had hoped they would be.

"You sound like my mother!" Keisha groaned. "*Keisha, eat your greens! Keisha, drink your milk! Keisha, you've had enough sweets for one day!* She's always bugging me."

"Besides, we already eat healthy lunches, Bernadette," added Annie.

"But we don't really know what vitamins and stuff are in the food we're eating, do we?" asked Bernadette. "This would be a very scientific way of learning what makes food healthy."

"My mother makes me and Connor take vitamins every morning," said Megan. "I know there's A, B, and C in them. Maybe some other letters too."

"How many vitamins are there?" asked Annie. "Do we have to go through the whole alphabet?"

"I don't know, but if there are twenty-six vitamins, we're going to have to make some very big lunches!" Bernadette replied.

"Only *you* would think that it's fun to turn lunchtime into a science lesson, Bernadette," said Keisha, in a very grumpy voice. "Lunch is supposed to be a break from school, not another science class."

"Does everyone think this is a bad strategy?" Bernadette asked. She wondered why Keisha was in such a bad mood.

"No, I like it," said Annie. "Because I like big lunches."

"I like it too," said Megan. "Because I never know what I want for lunch when my mother asks me the night before, so *any* strategy is a good strategy."

"OK, OK. If you guys really want to do this I will too," said Keisha. "But I sure hope I can find a good dessert with some stupid vitamins in it."

Annie did have a very big lunch that Friday. Her mother had helped her make a stir-fry full of healthy ingredients. The other girls tried to identify them all.

"You have carrots for vitamin A, Annie," said Megan. "I brought carrots today too. Actually, I bring carrots *every* day because I love them. So does my hamster, Mr. McWhiskers."

"I see some broccoli and my mother says that broccoli has almost all the important vitamins," said Bernadette. "Which is why she makes me eat it, even though I only like the pretty flower tops and not the tough old tree trunks. But what are all those little white cubes in your noodles, Annie?"

"Tofu," said Annie. "It's made out of soybeans. And it's full of vitamin E and protein, in case you were wondering."

"There are some red peppers, so I see vitamin C," Megan added.

"Too bad they're not frozen, because 'I see icy C' would make a great tongue-twister," said Keisha. She then said it three times herself, very fast.

"You and your tongue-twisters!" Annie groaned. "I thought once the Christmas pageant was over you would stop practicing them!"

"Did you know that all red and orange vegetables have vitamin C?" said Bernadette.

"Then *you* must be full of vitamin C, Bernadette, because your hair is really red!" sang Annie.

"Ha ha, very funny," said Bernadette, twirling one of her long pigtails. Something silver glittered

on her wrist, and Megan reached out and grabbed
it to see what it was.

"Ooh, I like your new bracelet," said
Megan. "Did you get it for Chanukah from your
grandparents?"

"No, it's a friendship bracelet," said Bernadette

proudly, showing it to all the girls. "Jasmine and I each got one at the Science Center. We're never ever going to take them off because we are going to be friends forever."

Nobody said anything for a moment.

"You didn't get friendship bracelets with *us*, Bernadette," said Keisha, looking at Megan meaningfully. "I guess that means we're not going to be friends forever, doesn't it? But I should have known that, because you didn't even bother to return my phone call last Friday."

"I'm sorry," said Bernadette. "I was just really, really busy. Maybe we can do it this weekend instead. I'll ask my mom when I get home."

"Oh, don't worry. We had the sleepover anyway, *without* you. And it was a ton of fun!" said Keisha.

Bernadette was so shocked that she didn't know what to say. Even though she'd had a good time without the Lunch Bunch, she wasn't happy to hear that they were having a good time without her! But she didn't have a chance to think of a response because their teacher, Mrs. Hawthorn, was walking around the lunchroom to make sure the students were behaving. She asked what the Lunch Bunch Strategy was that week and when Annie told her, she said she was impressed. She said good nutrition was important, especially for growing children, and since nutrition was already on the curriculum, maybe the whole class should participate in a Healthy Food Challenge.

Keisha groaned. "Bernadette will love that. Now she'll get to lecture the whole class instead of just the Lunch Bunch."

"I wasn't lecturing anyone, Keisha," Bernadette protested.

"How would the Healthy Food Challenge work, Mrs. Hawthorn?" asked Megan, trying to change the topic. She hated it when people argued.

"I'll have to think about it. But maybe I could

give out stickers to whoever in my class brings a healthy lunch to school, or brings a note from home proving that they ate a healthy lunch there, and the person with the most stickers at the end of the month will get a special prize."

"I hope the *prize* isn't going to be healthy too, Mrs. Hawthorn," Keisha said. "Make it something tasty like a chocolate bar instead. Please?"

"Well, Valentine's Day is coming up," said Mrs. Hawthorn. "So chocolate might be appropriate."

"You thought it was weird that I turned lunch into a science lesson, Keisha. But that's not as strange as you turning a healthy food challenge into a way to get chocolate," said Bernadette, trying to get Keisha to laugh.

"I never pass up a chance to eat chocolate," said Keisha.

But she wasn't even smiling.

5

Elastic Annie

A *lot* of students stopped smiling when they heard about the Healthy Food Challenge. They didn't mind learning about how many portions of fruits and vegetables, grains, and protein they should eat each day. Mrs. Hawthorn handed out black and white illustrations of a healthy plate to help them remember. It was fun coloring in all the fruits and vegetables, although there weren't enough different shades of brown and beige crayons to make bread and pasta and rice look interesting—or appetizing.

They also liked bringing in their favorite recipes and talking about the ingredients needed to make them. The best class of all was when they actually got to cook something at school. First Mrs. Hawthorn read them a story called *Stone Soup*. The next day, each student had to bring something: a few carrots, potatoes or onions; salt, pepper, basil or oregano; or a can of tomatoes. Mrs. Hawthorn brought in a big electric pot and plugged it in so they could make stone soup themselves (it was really just vegetable soup with a "magic" stone sitting on the bottom of the pot), and then they ate it. The principal, Mrs. Garcia, brought in some delicious bread and shared in their feast.

But most of the time it was harder to *eat* healthy food than to talk about it. It was especially hard to bring something from every single food group to lunch every single day! Some people said they couldn't because they had allergies. And some people said they wouldn't because they hated vegetables, or milk, or were vegetarian. And a whole lot of people were mad at Bernadette because they thought that the Healthy Food Challenge was her idea.

Bernadette told anyone who would listen that it *wasn't* her idea; she had just made up the strategy for one single lunch, and Mrs. Hawthorn decided to copy it for the class for a whole month. But nobody believed her.

"The Lunch Bunch is famous for making up weird meals, Bernadette," explained Jackie Renfrew, the boy who sat next to her. "And people know you started the Lunch Bunch. So they think that you gave the idea of the Healthy Food Challenge to Mrs. Hawthorn."

"Well, she said we had to study nutrition this year anyway! So all she borrowed from the Lunch Bunch was the idea of having a strategy," Bernadette protested.

"I don't mind, Bernadette," Jackie said. "I'm having fun."

"I'm not. I hate being blamed for something I didn't do!" She felt like crying.

"Don't worry about the complainers. They're just sulky," said Jackie.

"What do you mean?" asked Bernadette.

"That's what my grandpa says when my sister starts whining about stuff. He says she's just sulky and needs a distraction. Usually he plays cards with her and that cheers her up."

"We can't play cards in class, Jackie," said Bernadette.

"I know. But maybe you could find a different kind of distraction."

After talking with Jackie, Bernadette felt a little better. She started scribbling in secret code in her green notebook, trying to come up with a good distraction. But since all she could think of were science experiments and what people were sulky about was a kind of science experiment, none of her ideas seemed distracting enough.

Luckily for her, something exciting was announced that made a very good distraction indeed: The Junior Gymnastics Competition. Not only were three students from Garden Road Elementary School—including Annie Wang—competing in the event, but it would be taking place at the school itself, the first week of February.

"Is it going to be like the Olympics, Annie?" asked Bernadette. "With judges holding up your score? And contestants bursting into tears? And loud music, and people throwing flowers, and everybody's parents going crazy?"

"Yes, it'll be *exactly* like that!" Annie replied.

"Does your team wear a uniform?" asked Megan. "Like my Brownie troop does?"

"Well, our jackets are kind of like a uniform, because they have our team name on them," Annie replied. "But we get brand new costumes for every competition."

"Does your costume have sparkles?" asked Keisha, who was very fond of sparkles. She had pierced ears and often wore sparkly little earrings. She had a blue pair, and a pink pair, and one pair that looked like real diamonds.

"This year it does. You would love my new leotard, Keisha! It's dark green with silver swoops across the front."

"It sounds beautiful!" said Keisha. "I wish I had a leotard like that."

"It sounds like a superhero costume, Annie. All you need is a cape," said Bernadette.

"Annie needs a superhero name to go with her superhero costume," said Megan. "Maybe we should call her 'Gymnastics Girl.'"

"How about 'Elastic Annie'? Because she's so flexible," Keisha suggested.

"You're so smart, Keisha! That's a perfect name

for her," said Bernadette. She was trying really hard to say nice things to Keisha these days so that her friend wouldn't be mad at her anymore.

"Yeah, my mom doesn't think you have any bones in your body, Annie. She says that you're made out of rubber," said Keisha.

"I wish I really *were* made out of rubber," said Annie. "Then I wouldn't be covered in bumps and bruises all the time. But I like the idea of being a superhero. So if you want to call me Elastic Annie, you have my permission."

Once the posters for the competition went up around the school, a lot of kids wanted to learn gymnastics. So one day, Mr. McGregor, the gym teacher, asked Annie to give the class a demonstration of some of the tricks she knew how to do.

First she did a cartwheel.

"I can do that too!" said a girl named Margaret, who was kind of a show-off. "It's no big deal."

Then Annie did a series of perfect cartwheels all around the gym without even stopping.

"Wow!" said Jackie Renfrew.

Next, she did a different kind of cartwheel landing on both feet. That was called a round-off. Then she did a really scary kind of cartwheel where she didn't even put her hands on the ground. And that was called an aerial.

A few of the kids gasped when she landed. Mr. McGregor reminded everyone immediately that Annie had years of practice and that they shouldn't try tricks like that on their own.

"Well, can you teach us how to do some tricks that *aren't* dangerous, Mr. McGregor?" asked Keisha. "I want to become elastic, just like Annie!"

"What about tumbling? Everyone likes that, and it's pretty safe," said Annie.

Mr. McGregor said, "Sure, Annie, that's a great idea."

He disappeared into the equipment room and

came out with a big blue mat. Then he went back and got another one. He unrolled both mats so that they made a soft surface on the gym floor, and then he asked Annie to demonstrate the proper form for front rolls and back rolls. All the children in the class took turns rolling around and laughing like crazy.

"It's a lot harder than it looks, Annie!" puffed Megan.

"You're taller than me. That means you have longer arms and legs to get tangled up in," Annie explained.

"Gee, maybe I should switch to gymnastics from science," said Bernadette. "I didn't realize that being short could be an advantage in anything."

"Everything is an advantage in something, and a disadvantage in something else," said Mr. McGregor. "For example, I have such big feet that I'm a terrible dancer. I step on my poor wife's toes all the time. But I'm a fantastic swimmer, because my feet are practically flippers."

"I don't think you can blame your bad dancing on your feet, Mr. McGregor!" laughed Keisha. "My father has *huge* feet and he's a great dancer."

"Well, it's the best excuse I've ever come up with, so I'm sticking to it," said Mr. McGregor. "Also, I believe that everything in life has a good and a bad side. It all depends on how you look at things."

Gymnastics had a good side and a bad side, as far as Bernadette was concerned. The good side was that it was fun, and a big distraction—for a couple of weeks anyhow. The kids in her class stopped complaining about the Healthy Food Challenge and started worrying about whether they would be able to do a handstand, or walk along the balance beam without falling off. The bad side was that she wasn't very good at gymnastics herself, even though she was almost as short as Annie.

"Rats!" she exclaimed when she could not push herself up from the floor into a bridge. "I look like a sick spider."

Annie burst out laughing. "I thought you knew all about insects, Bernadette! Spiders have *eight* legs, not four."

"Number one: I know spiders have eight legs; I was just trying to be funny. And number two, I *do* know all about insects, which is why I know that spiders aren't insects."

"They're not?"

"No. Insects have six legs, and antennas." Bernadette wiggled two fingers in front of her forehead.

"Lobsters have antennas. Are they insects?" asked Jackie Renfrew.

"Not exactly, but they are related," said Bernadette.

"TVs have antennas. Are they insects?"

asked Keisha, who seemed to have finally for-
given Bernadette for being rude to her over the
Christmas holidays.

"Ha ha," said Bernadette. "Good one!" She
gave Keisha a high five, and they smiled at each
other.

"You know so much about science, Bernadette.
You shouldn't worry about whether or not you can
do gymnastics," Annie said.

"My friend Jasmine is good at science *and*
sports," said Bernadette, "so I know it's possible
to be good at both."

"Well, we all know that Jasmine's good at
everything," said Keisha, suddenly angry at
Bernadette all over again. "In fact, she's *perfect*."

"I didn't say that, Keisha!"

"Whatever," said Keisha, walking over to
where Megan was practicing backwards rolls.

Bernadette watched her walk away. She felt so
stupid. Why did she bring up Jasmine's name just

when Keisha seemed ready to be friends again? Life was just too complicated! She had already apologized for not calling Keisha back. She had stopped calling Jasmine her "best" friend. Now it seemed like Keisha didn't want her to ever mention Jasmine at all—but that wasn't fair, was it? Keisha talked about her camp friends sometimes, and nobody got mad at *her*.

If Bernadette thought she was in the doghouse before, things were even worse now. Although the Lunch Bunch had stopped planning their Friday strategies to concentrate on the Healthy Food Challenge, they still sat together at lunchtime. But as soon as the meal was over, Annie ran off to the gym to practice with the other two kids who were going to be in the Junior Gymnastics Competition. And sometimes Keisha and Megan wandered off to recess by themselves, holding hands, instead of waiting for Bernadette. Bernadette knew that

Keisha and Megan had been friends for years. They'd been doing things together long before the Lunch Bunch existed, so there was no rule that said they *had* to include the others in everything they did. But it still hurt her feelings when they left her out.

The worst time was when Keisha and Megan talked during lunch about how much fun they had at a sleepover that weekend. Annie wasn't allowed to go to Saturday night sleepovers because she had gymnastics practice early Sunday morning, so it didn't bother her. But Bernadette was very upset that she hadn't been invited to join them. She swallowed hard, and then broke into the conversation.

"Hey guys," she said. "After Annie's finished her competition, we should all have a sleepover at *my* house. We can make a fort in the basement and sleep in it like we did at my pirate party."

"I can't wait!" said Annie. "I'm so sick of not being able to do anything on the weekends."

"What a great idea!" said Megan, with a happy smile. "Won't that be fun, Keisha? The Lunch Bunch all together again?"

"Maybe," said Keisha. She didn't sound very enthusiastic, but Bernadette reminded herself that "maybe" was more than halfway to "yes."

The day of the Junior Gymnastics Competition, Bernadette, Keisha, and Megan all showed up to cheer for Annie. So did Jackie Renfrew, who asked shyly if he could sit with them. Keisha said of course he could, and immediately slid along the bench so that Jackie could fit in the space between her and Bernadette. Bernadette didn't say anything, but secretly, she was kind of happy to have Jackie at her side because she knew he would talk to her and she wasn't sure whether Keisha would. Of course, once the competition began, everyone started yelling and clapping like crazy and it was impossible to have a conversation anyway.

It was especially exciting when it was Annie's turn to compete. Bernadette was so proud of her! No matter how hard Annie's tricks were she never stopped smiling. She walked along the balance beam as gracefully as a bird, and then did a back

flip, landing on the narrow beam without even a wobble. She did a handstand that turned into a forward roll. And when she finished her routine, she turned and waved at her friends before running off to sit with her team at the side of the gymnasium.

"Oooh, I hope Annie wins!" said Bernadette.

"Me too," said Jackie Renfrew.

"I love her costume," said Keisha. "She really *does* look like a superhero. A tiny superhero without a cape."

"A tiny superhero made completely out of elastic!" said Megan, laughing.

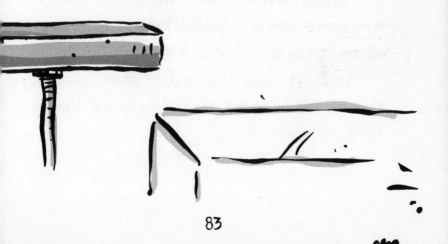

Elastic Annie's team came in third all around and Annie herself came second in the exercises on the beam. Her grandmother couldn't stop crying, and her father gave her a beautiful bouquet of flowers. Then Bernadette, Megan, and Keisha ran over and gave her so many hugs she disappeared underneath them.

"Valentine's Day isn't until next week!" Annie squeaked. "Save some of the love for then!"

"My mom always says the more love you give away, the more you have left," said Megan.

"That's so beautiful, Megan," said Bernadette. "I wonder if it's true."

"It may be true of love," said Keisha. "But I wish it were true of chocolate! Because I'm giving all my friends chocolate for Valentine's Day."

And everyone laughed at that, except Bernadette. She wasn't sure if she was still one of Keisha's friends.

6

A New Strategy

At Garden Road Elementary School, Valentine's Day was a lot of fun. Every class made a mailbox so that students could send greetings and candy to their friends. Some people, like Megan, made their own cards with construction paper, and doilies, and ribbons, and glitter, and glue. Some people, like Bernadette, preferred to buy cards with pictures of cute puppies on them. Some people, like Annie, went for cards with funny jokes, riddles, and puzzles. And others people, like Keisha, gave their friends chocolate hearts wrapped in shiny pink paper because chocolate tastes a lot better than cards do.

But this Valentine's Day was going to be different, because it was also the day the class would find out the winner of the Healthy Food Challenge. A few kids were excited because they thought they might win. Other kids were just sick of studying nutrition and were looking forward to a new science unit about weather, or electricity, or endangered animals. So everyone paid attention when Mrs. Hawthorn greeted the class that morning.

"Happy Valentine's Day, Grade Three!" she said. "I'm just going to sort out all your cards and distribute them. Then, after you've had a chance to read your valentines, I'll announce the winner of the Healthy Food Challenge."

"I hope it's me," said Bernadette. "Otherwise I ate a lot of broccoli for nothing."

"You keep saying that you hate broccoli, Bernadette, but you never look unhappy when you're eating it," Megan said.

"It's not really *that* bad . . . but please don't tell my mother! She still thinks she has to reward me for eating my vegetables. I've got a good deal going," said Bernadette.

"This is so weird," said Annie, who was looking through her valentines.

"What is?" said Megan.

"I got a card with a poem on it, and it's signed 'a secret admirer'!"

"Wow, a mystery," said Bernadette. "I totally *love* mysteries. Let me see it, Annie! I'll bet I can figure out who it's from."

Annie handed over a neatly typed piece of paper. It read:

Annie Wang is fantastic,

Her body's made out of elastic.

A secret admirer

"Hmm. Whoever this is knows how to rhyme well," said Bernadette. "So that's our first clue."

"Ha!" said Megan. "It actually sounds a lot like this valentine my brother Connor gave me this morning."

"What did his valentine say?" asked Annie.

Megan held it up. It read:

Roses are red

Pickles are green

My face is funny

But yours is a scream.

"I hate to disappoint you, Megan, but Connor doesn't sound like a secret admirer," said Keisha.

"Anyhow, who do you think sent this card to Annie?"

"I know *exactly* who it is," said Bernadette. "It's Jackie Renfrew." She walked over to where he was sitting and poked him in the arm.

"How did you know it was me?" said Jackie. He was blushing so much that his freckles blended together into a red streak across his nose and cheeks.

"It was easy, Jackie! You were so busy listening to what we were saying that you didn't even look at your *own* valentines. Meanwhile, everybody else in the class has opened all of theirs."

"I didn't know you were a great detective as well as a great scientist, Bernadette!" Jackie laughed.

"Well, they're kind of the same thing, aren't they? Both detectives and scientists try to solve mysteries by studying clues."

"I never thought of that before," said Jackie.

"Anyhow, I didn't know that *you* were a great poet as well as a great musician, Jackie," said Bernadette. (Jackie Renfrew played violin better than anyone else in the school, even the big kids.)

"Well, they're kind of the same thing too, aren't they? Because poetry is like music, except with words," said Jackie.

"If there was a poetry competition like my gymnastics competition, Jackie, you would definitely be a winner," said Annie, giving him a hug.

"Jackie's already a winner," said Mrs. Hawthorn, who was walking around the classroom with a basket to collect the envelopes for recycling. "I'm pleased to announce that Jackie Renfrew has won this class's Healthy Food Challenge."

"I did?" Jackie was amazed.

"Come up to the front of the class and collect your prize."

Jackie went up to the front of the class where Mrs. Hawthorn gave him a box wrapped in red paper. He ripped the paper open carefully. Inside the box were four little chocolate cupcakes with white frosting and pink sprinkles on top.

"I'm going to take these treats home to share with my little sister, OK?" said Jackie.

"Good idea," said Mrs. Hawthorn. "Now close that box before anyone else gets too interested!"

"I'm glad it was you, Jackie," said Annie, when he came and sat down again. "Because I've never had a secret admirer before!"

"I wish I had a secret admirer," said Keisha with a sigh.

"You have *lots* of admirers," said Bernadette. "Remember the Christmas pageant? Everyone clapped the most for you, because you are such a good actress."

"Hmm," said Keisha, shrugging.

"*I* admire you, Keisha."

"Really? Not enough to give me a friendship bracelet, though," said Keisha. "Not enough to return my phone calls. Not enough to want me to play with Jasmine. I wouldn't call that *admiring* me, Bernadette."

"You two have to stop fighting," said Megan. "It makes me so sad. I *want* to have a sleepover at Bernadette's house, Keisha, even if you don't. I want everything to be the way it was before!"

"Who says we're fighting?" Keisha replied. "Fighting means yelling and screaming, doesn't it? I don't hear anyone yelling and screaming, do you?"

"Come on, it's obvious," Annie broke in. "You don't have to be a detective to tell when people are mad at each other! And it's silly for you to be mad at each other because you two are such good friends. We're *all* good friends. We're the LUNCH BUNCH!"

"I *thought* that we were good friends," said Keisha, "but Bernadette likes Jasmine better than she likes the rest of us."

"I do not like her better than I like you guys!" said Bernadette.

"Yes, you do. As soon as she showed up, you made it clear that we weren't important to you anymore."

"Is there a problem over here, girls?" asked Mrs. Hawthorn. "Because it's time to pack up your knapsacks and go home. Didn't you hear the bell ring?"

"Sorry, Mrs. Hawthorn," said Keisha. "My sister Monique is probably waiting for me in the school yard already."

And she left the room without saying good-bye.

By the time Bernadette got outside, Keisha had already gone. Sometimes Keisha and her big sister Monique and her little brother Joshua still walked home with Bernadette and her mother, but today wasn't going to be one of those days. Now that

Bernadette thought about it, there had been fewer and fewer of those days recently. She couldn't even remember the last time they'd written an entry in their dog-watching book.

"Bernadette Inez O'Brian Schwartz, you're awfully quiet," her mother said. "I thought you'd have all kinds of stories to tell me about Valentine's Day! Did everybody like your cute puppy cards?"

"Yup."

"And wasn't today supposed to be the day you found out who won the Healthy Food Challenge?"

"Yup. Jackie Renfrew won."

"What was the prize?"

"Four little chocolate cupcakes."

"Hmmm. That doesn't sound very healthy to me! Was there zucchini in the cupcakes? Because I have a good recipe for chocolate-zucchini muffins we can make this weekend, if you want to invite some of your friends over."

"I'm not sure who my friends are anymore," said Bernadette sadly.

"What do you mean? What's going on?"

"I'm in the doghouse, Mom."

"Is there anything I can do?" asked Bernadette's mother. She was so worried that she stopped walking and Bernadette almost bumped into her.

"No, thanks," Bernadette answered. "This is not one of those problems a mother can solve."

"The older you get, the fewer problems I can solve for you, Bernadette. But I'm always here if you want to talk. Sometimes just saying things out loud can help."

"If I need to talk I'll let you know. But right now, what I need to do is *think*."

For Bernadette, this type of thinking usually meant staring out the window for a while, and then making some hot chocolate, and then playing with her guinea pig, Hamlet, and then re-organizing her fossil collection.

"You do whatever you have to do, Bernadette," said her mom, giving her a big hug. "I don't know anyone better than you at figuring out the solutions to problems."

When Bernadette got home she went to the living room and moved a giant pile of newspapers and magazines off the sofa, found a fuzzy blanket and a big pillow, and made herself a warm nest to curl up in next to the window. First she blew on the window until it fogged up, and then she scratched a question mark on it with her fingernail. Then she wiped the question mark away and looked outside. The snow sculptures she made with Jasmine were still in the backyard, though their shapes weren't as clear as they had been six weeks before. Instead of a snow dog chasing a snow cat chasing a snow mouse, there was a **BIG** pile of snow chasing a **smaller** pile of snow chasing a tiny pile of snow. Bernadette sat there for a long time watching the piles of snow chase each other around and around the yard. And her thoughts went around and around with them.

Six weeks before, she and Jasmine were out there playing together. They'd had so much fun! It wasn't fair that Keisha was mad at her for having fun with somebody else, somebody she hadn't seen since the summer. Bernadette only had three days with Jasmine; she got to play with Keisha all the time. So why was Keisha jealous? Because Keisha was mean. Even though she looked so pretty and sparkly and made the funniest jokes in the world, deep down inside she was a really truly *mean* person.

Bernadette decided she wouldn't be friends with Keisha anymore.

But that wouldn't work. Bernadette knew she would miss Keisha just as much as she missed Jasmine. Probably even more, because even though Jasmine had moved away, she was still Bernadette's friend, but Keisha would be sitting right there, in class, *not* being her friend. Bernadette's heart was already sore. She didn't want to feel that way forever.

Besides, if Bernadette wasn't friends with Keisha anymore she couldn't be friends with Megan either, because Keisha and Megan had been friends forever, so Megan would stick with Keisha even if it meant hurting Bernadette's feelings. And that meant she would lose *two* friends. And without those two friends, there wouldn't be any more Lunch Bunch.

She could probably still eat lunch with Annie, sometimes. But Annie and Bernadette would just be two people, and there was no way that two people could be called a "bunch"! Or maybe Annie wouldn't want to eat with her either, because it would be too awkward to leave her other friends, and then Bernadette would be stuck sitting with Jackie Renfrew, just like she had at the beginning of the school year. Jackie Renfrew was way more interesting than Bernadette thought when she first met him, but he wasn't as interesting as the Lunch Bunch.

For example, he wasn't as funny as Keisha. *No one* was as funny as Keisha.

Thinking so much about lunch made Bernadette hungry, so she went to the kitchen to make hot chocolate. First she took out her special china mug with a picture of a puppy on it, and put in one teaspoon of cocoa powder and two teaspoons of sugar. Then she filled the mug halfway with milk and stirred up the mixture. When the powder had started to dissolve, she filled the mug the rest of the way with milk and put it in the microwave for exactly one minute and ten seconds. If she put it in longer it would boil over and make a big mess, but if she put it in for a shorter time the cocoa would just float on top of the milk like mud in a puddle.

Bernadette dropped a handful of miniature marshmallows into her cocoa and watched them melt. When they had blended into a single layer, it was time to drink the cocoa. Well, that was the way *Bernadette* liked to drink her cocoa. Annie had a different strategy; she liked to stir her cocoa with a peppermint stick so it absorbed the minty flavor, and then take little bites out of the candy while she drank. Keisha was a big fan of dipping graham crackers in her cocoa because that reminded her of eating s'mores at summer camp. And Megan preferred hot milk with a drop or two of vanilla in it instead of cocoa. Each girl in the Lunch Bunch had her own special way of doing things—her own special talents, her own special tastes.

Bernadette put down her empty mug and went to get Hamlet. As soon as he heard her coming, he stood up on his hind paws and put his front ones up on the gate, asking to be picked up. He was always so happy to see her that she felt guilty for leaving him in his cage all day long, like a fluffy little prisoner waiting to be let out of jail. But whenever he got tired of playing, he waddled right back to the cage, squeaking to be put back inside. So obviously his cage didn't seem like a prison to *him*. It was his very own house; a house full of yummy things to eat, a soft bed of hay, and a tube to climb through. Hamlet might be her pet, but he was also himself. He had his own feelings too, which you could understand if you paid attention to him.

"*Whee!*" said Hamlet.

"I'm glad you're so happy to see me," said Bernadette. "Because nobody else is these days."

"*We,*" Hamlet said again, firmly.

"Yes, we will always be friends." said Bernadette.

"*Week?*" Hamlet asked.

"What about this week? I don't understand," Bernadette replied.

"*Week, week!*" Hamlet insisted.

"You're absolutely right!" said Bernadette. "We're supposed to make a new strategy for lunch this week, now that the Healthy Food Challenge is finally over! But we forgot to plan one for this Friday."

She gave Hamlet a ride on her skateboard around the living room just for fun, and then fed him two strawberries for being such a big help. Strawberries were his favorite treat. Bernadette

knew what Hamlet liked to eat because she loved him, and he knew that she loved him because she gave him his favorite things to eat.

Everything made sense to Bernadette now. She knew exactly what she had to do.

The next day was Wednesday, so there wasn't much time to think of another strategy if this one didn't work. Luckily, Annie and Megan *loved* Bernadette's idea, and Keisha didn't say she wouldn't participate. So even though her heart still hurt every time Keisha ignored her or Megan gave her a sad look, Bernadette just concentrated on doing her school work, and helping Jackie Renfrew with his math. And then it was Friday, the Lunch Bunch's special day, and time for each girl to show what she had brought.

"I made lunch for Annie today, which is why I have this gigantic lunch box," said Megan. "We all know that Annie's favorite meal is soup. So I brought her a Thermos of minestrone. And also crackers and cheese, and celery, and olives, and a hard-boiled egg with a tiny shaker of salt, because I didn't think that soup alone would be enough to fill Elastic Annie's hollow leg. I also brought her grape juice to drink, and a slice of banana bread and a bunch of grapes for dessert."

"Wow!" said Annie. "You can make lunch for me any time, Megan. You thought of all my favorite things."

"This was a great strategy, Bernadette," said Megan. "I can't wait to see what Keisha made me for *my* lunch!"

"Well, it wasn't that hard to figure out, Megan. I made you a poppy seed bagel with cream cheese and strawberry jam on it, because you always order that when we go out for a snack after choir practice," said Keisha. "And I gave you milk to drink. And a lot of carrot and celery sticks, of course. I even put in a few extra for Mr. McWhiskers. And for dessert, you have a crunchy green apple and three of my mom's famous ginger cookies, because I know how much you love them."

"Yummy!" cried Megan, so loudly some people at the next table turned around to see what was going on. "This is the best lunch *ever*."

"What did you make me, Annie?" asked Bernadette.

"I made you two mini-pizzas on English muffins, and a little bag of cherry tomatoes, and a container of chocolate milk, and a can of peaches because real peaches always get squished. There is also a granola bar to save for recess snack," said Annie. "And I even drew a cartoon puppy on your napkin for you, just like your Mom always does. How did I do?"

"You got an 'A' in knowing Bernadette," said Bernadette. "It's pretty amazing how well we all know each other, isn't it? Do you want to know what I made for you, Keisha?"

"I'll bet you made me macaroni and cheese," said Keisha.

"Of course I did," answered Bernadette. "With ketchup on the side."

"And apple juice?"

"With a pink and white striped straw," said Bernadette. "And a container of sliced cucumbers with some Caesar dressing to dip them in, and a navel orange, and two chocolate sandwich cookies."

"Wow," said Keisha slowly. "I guess you *do* know me pretty well."

"That's because we're such good friends, Keisha. You may not be my oldest friend, but you are definitely one of my *best* friends."

Keisha was silent for a moment. Then she stood up and took her macaroni over to the microwave to heat it up. When she came back to where the other girls were sitting in uncomfortable silence, she speared some macaroni on her fork and dipped it carefully into the ketchup. Finally she looked up at Bernadette and asked, "Was this whole strategy about me, Bernadette?"

"Yes," said Bernadette. "I'm so sorry I hurt your feelings, Keisha. I didn't realize how much it hurt to feel ignored and left out until you did it back to me, but I've learned my lesson."

"Really?" said Keisha. "Because it wasn't just *my* feelings that got hurt, Bernadette. You need to apologize to Megan too. She felt the same way I did—that even though we invited you to become our friend when you were lonely, once Jasmine came for a visit, we weren't good enough for you anymore."

"But Megan, you never *said* anything!"

"I hate fighting with people," said Megan, starting to cry. "I just want us to stay friends forever."

Bernadette went over to Megan and gave her a big hug. She started crying a little bit too.

"What about me?" said Annie. "Don't *I* get a hug?"

"Are you mad at me too?" asked Bernadette, with a sad face.

"No," said Annie. "I just like hugging!"

Then all four girls got together in a giant group hug, and their tears turned to laughter. Once they sat down again to eat their lunches, Annie spoke up.

"I think *you* should apologize too, Keisha, for making such a fuss about Bernadette seeing an old friend for a few days. It almost broke up the Lunch Bunch."

"I'm sorry," said Keisha. "I didn't think about that."

"Anyhow, the whole idea of 'best' friends is silly," Annie continued. "Everyone is the best friend for *something*. We should have friends for skating with, and friends for swimming with, and friends for watching movies with, and friends for going to camp with."

"And friends for cooking with, and friends for making art with," added Megan.

"And friends for tickling, and friends for chasing!" shouted Keisha, making Tyrannosaurus Rex claws of her hands.

"And friends for running away from!" shouted Bernadette, running away.

"Bernadette Inez O'Brian Schwartz!" Mrs. Hawthorn called after her. "You come back here *this minute*. Lunch isn't over yet."

"You're right, Mrs. Hawthorn," said Bernadette. Then she turned to her friends. "And luckily, the Lunch Bunch isn't over yet either!"

7

The Not-So-Secret Garden

Once Bernadette was out of the doghouse, she and Keisha often walked to school together again. They also went back to work on their dog-watching list and added a few new names:

Sophie, German Shepherd, March 1st
Mango, Poodle, March 15th
Chewbacca, Bernese Mountain Dog,
April 4th

And soon winter turned into spring, and there were lots of other things besides dogs to look at. The girls often stopped to admire a blossoming tree or a pond full of goldfish, a sparrow splashing in a birdbath, or a row of green sprouts poking through the earth. In the spring, the whole city seemed to turn into a garden!

One place was not in bloom, however: Mrs. Marsh's front yard. Once the snow melted it was just a patch of mud and weeds. Kids were still throwing garbage into it, so at least once a week Bernadette and Keisha had to clean it up. Then one day, when Bernadette was walking home with her mother and Keisha and Joshua, Bernadette had a brilliant idea.

"Hey guys, I have a brilliant idea!" she said. "Mrs. Marsh liked it when we cleaned up her yard last fall. So I bet she'd love it even more if we planted flowers here this spring."

"Bernadette Inez O'Brian Schwartz!" said her mother. "Why didn't *I* think of that?"

"Can I help too?" asked Joshua. "I'm a good digger."

"You bet," said Bernadette's mother. "We couldn't possibly manage without you, Joshie!"

They came back that very weekend with two dozen little pots of pansies to plant all along the fence. They also spread grass seed over the muddy lawn, and pulled out all of the weeds.

"No one will ever want to throw garbage in here when they see how pretty it looks," said Bernadette with satisfaction, wiping her muddy hands on her pants.

"Bernadette!" cried her mother.

"Sorry, Mom," said Bernadette. "But you have to admit, this garden is worth doing a little extra laundry."

They continued weeding and watering until the new grass started coming in nice and green.

Bernadette was right: hardly anybody threw garbage in the yard after that. Best of all, to everyone's surprise, what looked like a spooky dead vine climbing up the front porch burst into bloom with beautiful pink roses.

"It's just like *The Secret Garden*—my favorite book," said Keisha.

"Except this garden is not so secret," added Bernadette.

For the whole month of May, the Not-So-Secret Garden was their special project. And since the weather was warm, Mrs. Marsh and Lady spent a lot of time sitting under the climbing roses, enjoying the fresh air and watching all the people come and go from the corner store next door.

Joshua wasn't afraid of Lady at all anymore. Sometimes he would sit next to the dog patting her, and he liked to help Bernadette and Keisha take her for a walk around the block. But one day, Lady wouldn't come with them. She started whining and scratching at the door to go into the house. Mrs. Marsh pulled herself up with her walker and said good-bye to the children. Her face looked worried.

"I think I'm going to have to take Lady to the vet," she said. "She's behaving so strangely."

"We'll come back tomorrow after school," said Bernadette. "Maybe Lady will feel more like going for a walk then."

But when they arrived the next day, neither Mrs. Marsh nor Lady was on the porch like they usually were. Joshua was upset.

"Is Lady sick?" he asked.

"I don't know, Joshie," Keisha answered.

"Pick me up so I can ring the doorbell and see if they're home," he insisted.

"I don't think we should," said Bernadette's mother. "If Mrs. Marsh wanted company, she'd be outside. So if she's *not* waiting for us, it must be because today isn't a good day for a visit."

"But remember what Mrs. Marsh told us the day we met her, Mom?" said Bernadette. "She said it's never rude to offer to help somebody. So she'll understand if we ring the bell just to see if everything's okay."

Bernadette's mother considered this for a moment. Then she said, "Just to see if everything is okay. We're not inviting ourselves in afterwards, Bernadette. We're going straight home."

But they didn't have to invite themselves in. Mrs. Marsh came *thump thump thumping* to the door at once and opened it in great excitement.

"Come to the kitchen, my dears, and see what a surprise my beautiful Lady has for you!"

And there, on the doggy bed next to Lady, were two tiny golden puppies with long silky ears. Their eyes weren't even open yet and they were making soft mewing sounds that made them sound more like cats than dogs.

"Look, Joshie, these doggies can't bite. They don't even have *teeth* yet!" said Keisha.

"I want one," he said. "Mrs. Marsh, can I have a puppy?"

"Joshua!" said Monique. "That's rude!"

"No, it isn't," said Mrs. Marsh. "But it is something you will need to talk to your parents about first. Lady and I are getting too old now to take care of puppies, so in a couple of months we will have to give them away to a good home—or two."

"We can be a good home, Mom, can't we? Please, Mom, *double* please with cherries on top? And even some broccoli to make it healthier?" Bernadette begged, trying to hug her mother and jump up and down at the same time.

"Maybe. We'll have to see what your father says," Bernadette's mother replied, but she was laughing.

And Bernadette laughed too, because she knew from experience that a "maybe," with laughter, was at least three quarters of the way to a "yes."

The end

About the Author

SUSAN GLICKMAN started writing about the adventures of Bernadette and her friends for her own children. *Bernadette in the Doghouse* is the sequel to *Bernadette and the Lunch Bunch*. Susan lives with her family, including Toby the dog, in Toronto.

About the Author